# 原來如此

文／王銘涵、孟瑛如
圖／謝慧珍
英文翻譯／吳侑達

他是我的同學天天，
明明看起來都跟我們
差不多，
但有時卻又跟我們有些
不一樣！

他也是我們班上的一份子，
卻總有些課沒有跟我們一起上！

他究竟是哪裡和我們不一樣，
為什麼可以不必上這些課呢？
我們一直想不明白……

聽說，
他有時候會到全國各地去比賽，
甚至還搭飛機到國外去參賽！
而且他還得過幾個很特別的獎呢！

上綜合課時，
老師要我們想想野外求生的方法，
天天想出好多種答案，
每一個答案都讓我們驚奇！

我們終於有些明白他的「不一樣」！

他常常有一些出乎意料之外的想法，
老師說：「愛迪生小時候也是這樣的，
大家要多跟天天學習。」

原來他就是所謂的「點子王」！

上數學課時，
老師在台上示範解題的方法，
天天一直舉手說自己還有別的解法，
而且不斷追問老師：「為什麼？」

我們都是只求算出答案就好，
他為什麼永遠在找新的解法？
這樣真的比較有趣嗎？

段考後，我偷偷看了他的分數，
他的成績好像也跟我差不多！

上體育課時，我喜歡跟天天打羽球，
因為他在課堂學習似乎是十項全能，
但在打羽球時卻常常會輸我，呵呵！

下課時，
我問天天要不要和我們一起玩躲避球，
他一口就答應了。

原來他也跟我們一樣喜歡玩躲避球！

天天生日時，
我和同學們合送了一張大卡片祝福他，
讓他好感動。

原來他也會大笑、大哭……

星期天，
我跟阿德一起
到天天家玩，
才知道原來他家
跟我家差不多。

我一直以為，
他爸媽一定很有錢
或是很有名，
所以他才會這麼厲害！

輔導室老師告訴我們：
「每個人的學習潛能都不一樣，
有些人能力好一點，
有些人能力弱一些，
但每個人都有他獨特存在的價值，
只要盡力做好自己就是發揮天賦潛能！」

老師還說：「天天是資優生，
他的某些表現會跟我們不太一樣，
有些課程內容必須為他加深、加廣，
所以他才要到資優班上課。
至於其他方面，
他跟大家都一樣，
並沒有什麼不同。」

原來如此！難怪有時在課堂上會看不到他。

資 優 生

他是天天，
他是資優生，
他跟我們大家一樣，
都在學校裡上課，
只是學習潛能比較特別，
有時需要到資優教室學習。

他是我們的同學，
我們喜歡跟他一起運動、一起遊戲與學習。

原來如此！我們終於明白了——

天天只是學習潛能比較特別，
他和我們都是一樣的！

　　當知道自己的孩子或學生被鑑定為資優生時，你曾經為自己的教學技巧或教育態度感到自豪嗎？或是因為自己未曾做過什麼而感到茫然？身為特教老師，在教育現場常聽到有人說：「資優生已是上天送給師長的禮物，為什麼還要占用別人的教育資源呢？」當下常不知如何向他們解釋。其實，只要是學生，都應該被照顧到其適性學習需求，就如同〈禮運大同篇〉所言：「人不獨親其親，不獨子其子，使老有所終，壯有所用，幼有所長，鰥寡孤獨廢疾者皆有所養。」只要是人，適性適才的發展是最基本的要求，制度上應盡可能協助每個人能活出最好的自己！

　　在教學生涯中，曾經遇過不少位資優生，可惜的是有時因為教師自身對資優教育的迷思，以至於未能及時發現孩子的優勢，總是在事過境遷後才徒留遺憾！其實每個人都有自己的學習特質，身為教育人員的我們，應該真正落實因材施教、有教無類，每個孩子本身的學習潛能與特質都該被重視，特殊教育的提供是資優生的權益而非特權。要看見每位學生的潛能特質，而非僅著眼於孩子的學習困難；要能看見每位學生的獨特點，幫助他開出最美麗的花朵或是長成大樹。千萬不要錯過學生重要的資優潛能開發期，才不會在學習階段結束時，在遺憾中與孩子們道再見。

　　若您身邊有資優生，不妨藉由此繪本在普通班做初步的特教宣導，讓同儕都能理解何謂「資優」或是「資優教育」，更可以進一步與校內的特教老師（資賦優異類）合作，為我們的資優生創造一個無障礙且能發揮所長的學習環境。

# So That Is How It Is!

**Written by Ming-Han Wang & Ying-Ru Meng**
**Illustrated by Houg-Jane Shieh**
**Translated by Arik Wu**

This is my classmate, Timmy.

He looks just like us,
but there seems to be something special about him!

For example, he is a member of our class,
but he gets to skip some classes.

Why is there such a difference? Why does he get to do that?
That is something we fail to understand!

We know that he gets to take part in competitions all around the country.

Sometimes, he even flies to participate in the ones held in other countries.

People say that he has won quite a few special awards over the past few years.

During scout training sessions, Teacher likes to ask us questions about how to survive in the wild.

Timmy always comes up with fascinating ideas!

Impressive! Now we start to see how special he is!

He is a perfect example of thinking outside the box.

Teacher tells us that Thomas Edison was also this type of person, and wants us to all learn from Timmy.

He is the idea hamster among us, so to speak.

During math classes, whenever Teacher tries to teach us how to solve math problems, Timmy always bombards her with a million "whys" and volunteers to demonstrate other possible ways of solving the problems.

Why bother? As long as we get it done, it is good enough. Why does he always have to look for alternative solutions?

Is it more interesting than getting it done in an instant?

I like to play badminton with Timmy during physical education classes.

He is near perfect when it comes to academic performance, but he is definitely not as good as I am when it comes to playing badminton! Hooray!

Here are the scores for our midterm exam! I take a peek at his.

Well, roughly the same as mine!

During one recess period, I ask Timmy if he wants to play dodgeball with us.

He says YES right away!

It turns out that he likes to play dodgeball as much as we do!


On his birthday, we make a large handmade birthday card for him. He looks so touched!

It turns out that he, just like us, is full of emotion!

One Sunday, Derek and I go visit Timmy at his home.

I used to think that his partents must be very famous and rich, but it turns out their house looks as plain as ours!

Intellectually gifted

A school counselor comes to teach us things about special education.

He says that different people have different potential.

Some people are born with greater potential, and some are not.

Still, every one of us has our own special calling, and we must live our lives to the fullest.

Teacher says that Timmy is intellectually gifted.

Some course materials are too easy for him, so he needs gifted education to better develop his potential.

Other than that, he is no different than any one of us.

So that is how it is! That is the reason why we do not see him in some class periods!

This is Timmy.

Indeed he is intellectually gifted, but he is also a member of our school.

The only difference is that he is a bit more special and is in need of gifted education.

He is our classmate! We love learning, playing, and doing exercise with him!

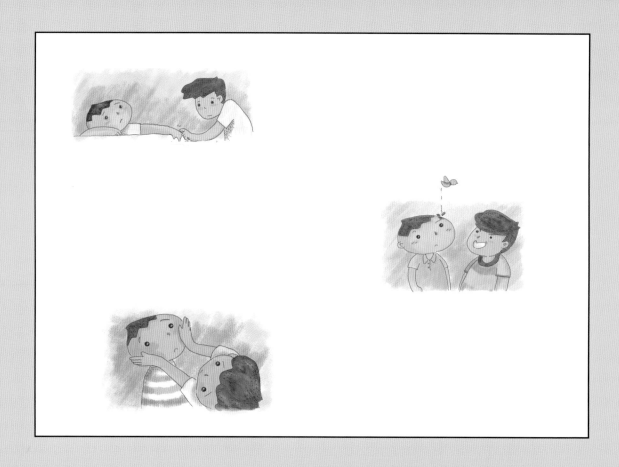

So that is how it is! Now we finally understand!

Timmy may appear more gifted than us on the outside - but deep down, he is just like us!